# Can I Play QUEENIE

### Jill Paton Walsh
### Illustrated by Jolyne Knox

THE BODLEY HEAD
LONDON

Gary's mother was expecting a baby quite soon. 'I'd like a girl this time,' she said.

'Why?' asked Gary. 'Don't you like boys?'

'I like you,' said mother. 'But I'm hoping to have one of each.'

'Why?' asked Gary. 'Why not two boys?'

'Well, you never know,' mother said. 'Perhaps two boys is what I'll get. That would save some money on clothes, anyway. Another boy could wear some of your things.' Mother had two big boxes of Gary's outgrown clothes to sort through.

'These are nice,' said Gary. He had found a tiny pair of dark green dungarees with teddy bears sewn on the pockets. 'Did I wear them?' He held up the green dungarees, and they only reached down as far as his waist.

'You have grown a bit,' said mother. 'You used to look nice in those.'

'A girl would look nice in them too,' said Gary.

'No,' said mother. 'A girl would rather have pretty things. Pink and lemon and pale blue T-shirts, and dresses, and little skirts.'

'Can we afford a girl?' asked Gary.

Mother laughed. 'You can't send people back!' she said. 'Whoever arrives is ours, girl or boy. But Rachel's mother has a big box of clothes that used to be Rachel's – if it's a girl we can have some of those. Don't worry.'

'We might have a big strong girl, with a bit of sense, who liked dungarees,' said Gary. 'After all, she's got me for a brother!'

'We might,' said mother. 'You can never tell with girls.'

'All my friends are boys,' Gary told her, as they folded up the clothes to put them away. 'It must be horrible being a girl.'

'I rather liked it, myself,' said mother.

At playtime the next day Gary was bored. He usually played with Peter and Robert, but today Robert was at the dentist, and Peter was away with a sore throat. All the other boys were playing French cricket, and Gary didn't like French cricket. He was always bowled out very quickly, and he liked things he was good at.

The girls were all playing
together at one end of the
playground. They were
shouting and laughing. They
seemed to be having a good
time. Gary went over to watch
them. Barbara saw him.
'What do you want?' she
asked fiercely.

'I want to play,' said Gary.

'This is a girls' game,' said Barbara.

'Why?' said Gary.

The girls stopped playing, and listened.

'It just is,' said Barbara. 'Anyone ever heard of a boy playing Queenie?'

'No!' the girls shouted.

'But *why*?' said Gary.

'Push off, Gary, we want to get on with it,' said Barbara.

'I know why you won't let me play,' said Gary. 'It's because I'd win all the time, that's why. It's because I'd beat you all rotten!'

'What makes you think you could beat us at our game?' said Barbara. She sounded very cross.

'Because boys are better at everything, that's why, frog-face!' said Gary.

'They're better at being rude and stupid, anyway,' said Barbara.

'Oh, go on, let him play,' said Alice. 'We'll soon see if he's any good.'

'Brilliant!' said Gary. 'What do I do?'

'Gorgon Bonnet!' said Barbara. 'He doesn't even know how to play!'

'Stand beside me, Gary,' said Alice. 'I'll show you.'

'Clare is Queenie,' said Alice. Clare went right up to the school wall, and stood facing it. She had a ball in her hand. Everyone else lined up about ten feet behind her.

'When she throws the ball, try to catch it,' said Alice.

Clare threw the ball high over her head, without looking round. It bounced. Nobody caught it. Everybody rushed for it, trying to get it. Penny got it.

'Now we hide it,' Alice told Gary, 'and we all pretend to have it.'

Gary made a fist in his pocket, so that it bulged as though it had a ball in it. 'That's good,' said Alice. She put her hands behind her back, as though she had something in them. Penny tucked the ball into the elastic of her shorts, in the small of her back. When they were all ready, they called to Clare:

*'Queenie, Queenie, who has the ball?*
*I haven't got it, it isn't in my pocket,*
*You can see, it isn't me,*
*Queenie, Queenie, who has the ball?'*

Clare turned round and looked at them all. She looked a good long time.

Then she said to Alice, 'Do a twizzle, Alice.'

Alice spun round, as quickly as she could. 'You have to do what she says,' she told Gary.

But of course, when she spun round Clare could see that Alice wasn't holding the ball behind her back.

'Lift your right arm, Gary,' Clare said. Gary had to take his hand out of his pocket to do that, and the bulge he had been making in his pocket disappeared.

'Penny,' said Clare, 'make a pair of scissors!'

'She has to open out her arms and legs like the shape of a pair of scissors,' said Alice.

Penny didn't jump her legs apart. She wriggled her sandals on the tarmac carefully, till her legs were wide astride. She didn't jump in case the ball popped out of her waistband. Nobody giggled or grinned while she did it, but she did it so carefully that Clare guessed.

'Penny!' she yelled. 'You've got it!'

'If she guesses right, she's still Queenie,' Alice told Gary. Penny threw the ball back to Clare, and they began again. The second time Lucy had the ball stuck up her shirt. Barbara was standing with her legs close together, pretending to have the ball held between her knees under her skirt. Everyone was pretending to have it except Lucy, who was looking bored. Gary had made his handkerchief into a ball, and stuffed it down his sock. Clare guessed wrong three times, so Lucy pulled out the ball, laughing, and Lucy was Queenie.

When Lucy threw the ball Gary caught it. 'Copped!' shouted Alice. 'Say, "Copped!", Gary.'

Catching the ball meant that Gary was Queenie. He threw the ball high and hard over his back, and waited. Then, when everyone chanted *'Queenie, Queenie, who has the ball?'* at him, he turned round and faced the row of girls.

There was a suspicious looking bump in Rachel's sweater. 'Do some jumps, Rachel,' Gary said. Rachel jumped up and down, but the bump didn't move. It wasn't made by a slippery rubber ball; perhaps she had screwed up a handkerchief and stuck it up her jumper.

Alice was looking very sly. She had turned up the collar of her denim jacket, and she was holding her head tipped back a bit . . . Perhaps she had the ball held between her collar and her neck. 'Do a handstand, Alice!' said Gary. Alice did a good one – she even walked three steps on her hands, but the ball didn't fall from her.

This wasn't as easy as Gary had thought. He made everyone do twizzles, and stretch arms and legs. But he couldn't see who had the ball. He had to just use his three guesses, and hope. He guessed Alice first; she was a big girl with layers of clothes on – a T-shirt, and a jacket, and a swingy sort of skirt. 'Oh, yes?' said Alice. 'Where have I got it, then, Gary? You have to say where.'

'It's in those frilly knickers you're wearing,' said Gary.

'How do you know what knickers I'm wearing?' said Alice.

'They showed when you did a handstand,' Gary said.

'Good try,' said Alice. 'But wrong, Gary. Sorry.'

Then he guessed Rachel — she was standing very stiff and straight, so perhaps she had the ball held between her knees somehow, even though he had made her jump, and do the scissors, and it hadn't fallen out.

'Where have I got it?' Rachel asked.

'It's in that purse thing you're wearing,' said Gary, hoping.

Everyone shouted 'NO!' again. 'Sorry, Gary,' said Rachel. 'It's the ball of wool for French knitting in here.'

'Oh, all right then!' said Gary. 'Barbara has it tied up in her scarf.'

But he was wrong again. It was looped in Clare's thick brown hair, and it hadn't fallen out even when he made her twizzle and jump.

So Clare would have been the next Queenie, except that the bell went for the end of break.

'Hard luck, Gary,' said Clare. 'We thought you wouldn't guess you can hide things in long hair . . . '

'No,' said Gary. 'My sister is going to have very short hair, and wear green dungarees.'

'Lucky thing!' said Clare. 'It takes ages having this lot brushed in the morning, and it hurts! My mum won't let me have it short.'

'Well, it does look a little bit nice, Clare,' said Gary. 'On you, I mean.'

In the line-up to go in for lessons Mike said to Gary, 'we all saw you, soapy dopsy, sissy missy, playing girls' games!'

But Gary didn't care. 'It was fun,' he said. 'Why should the girls have all the good fun?'

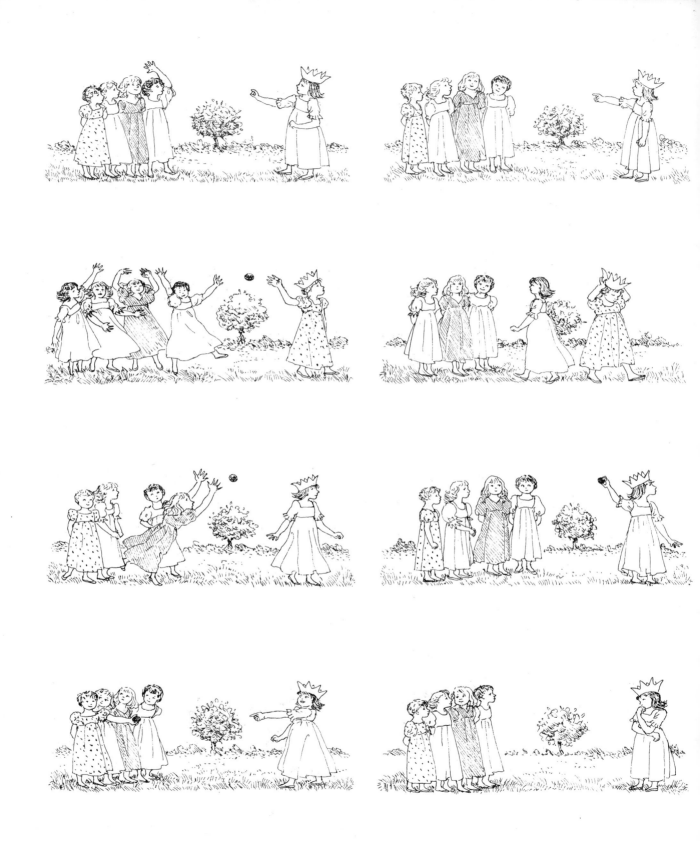